Huxley,
the Opry
House Mouse

Written By:
Amy Galofaro

Illustrated By:
Joshua Archote

AuthorHouse™
1663 Liberty Drive
Bloomington, IN 47403
www.authorhouse.com
Phone: 1 (800) 839-8640

Published by AuthorHouse 07/26/2018

ISBN: 978-1-5462-5036-4 (sc)
ISBN: 978-1-5462-5037-1 (e)

Library of Congress Control Number: 2018908058

Print information available on the last page.

This book is printed on acid-free paper.

authorHOUSE®

There is a wonderful place in the great state of Tennessee called Nashville. Nashville's nickname is Music City because a lot of people from near and far travel there to sing.

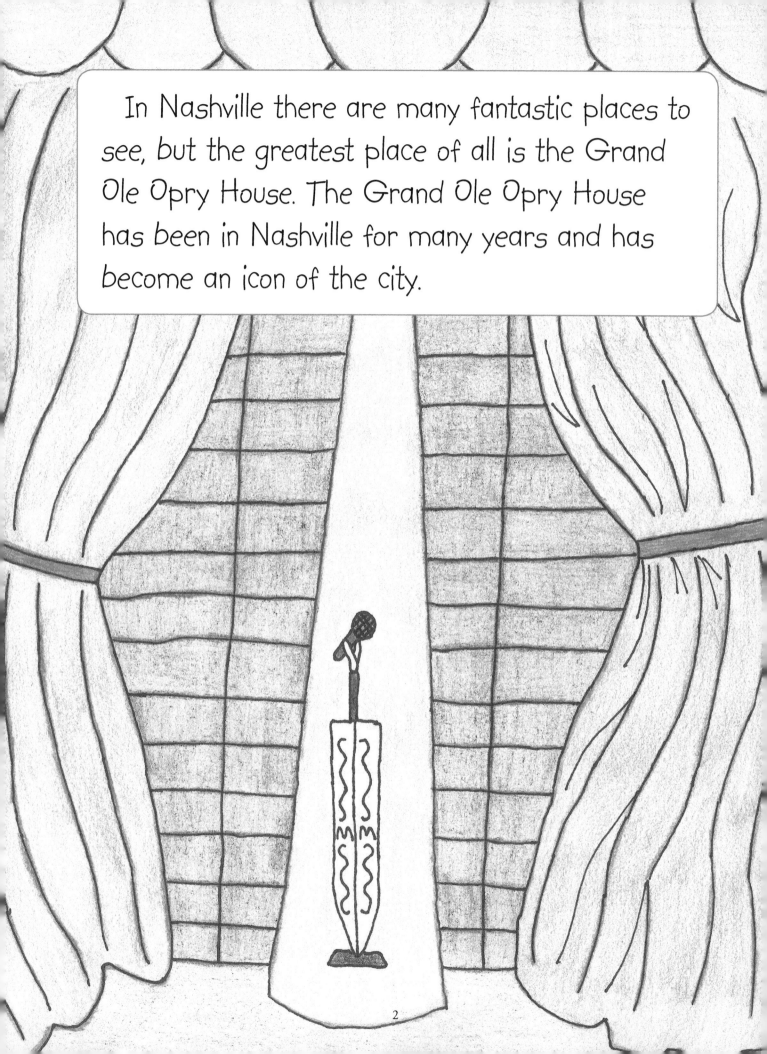

In Nashville there are many fantastic places to see, but the greatest place of all is the Grand Ole Opry House. The Grand Ole Opry House has been in Nashville for many years and has become an icon of the city.

Several nights a week there is a big show at the Grand Ole Opry House. Very talented country music singers perform on the legendary stage.

Hundreds of people fill the seats to cheer the singers on. Behind the stage, also watching the show each night, is a tiny mouse named Huxley.

Every night when the show ends, the big red curtain falls over the stage, and the seats empty, Huxley steps onto the stage.

Huxley used to sing with his friends on stage after the show. It usually took a few of them to pull the big ropes to open the curtain.

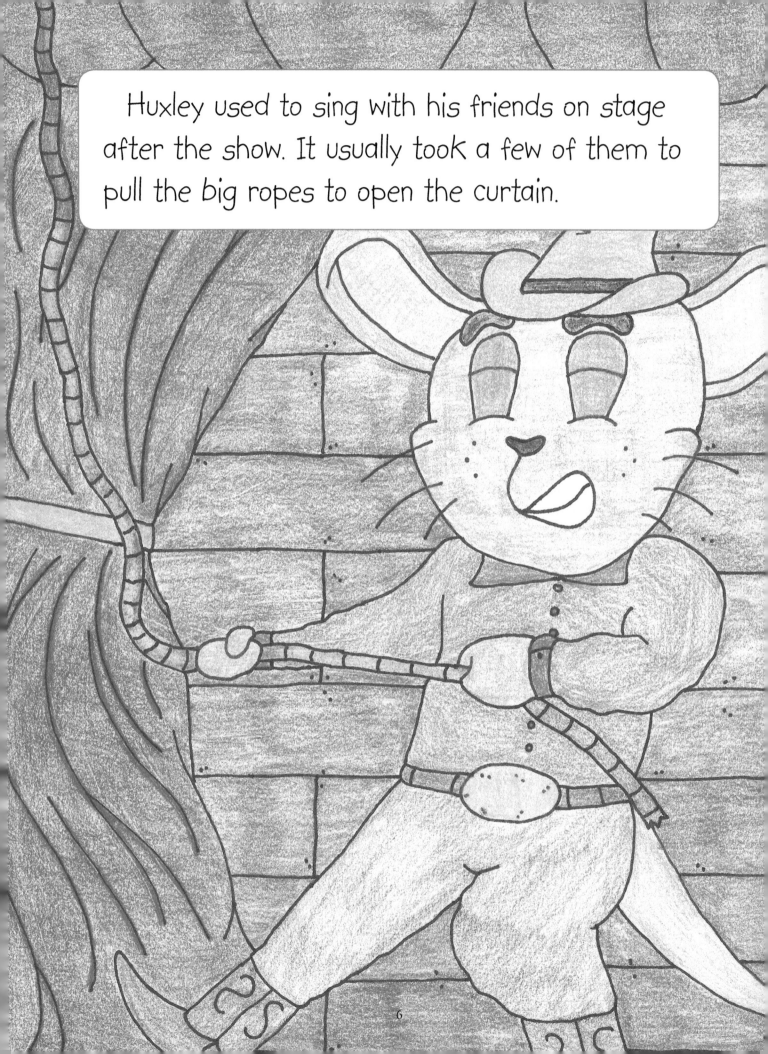

Huxley and his friends moved into the Opry House a year ago when they started a band. Each night they watched the show.

When there was no one there, the mice played their own music. Huxley loved playing his banjo and singing even if there was no one watching, but his friends did not feel the same way.

Huxley's friends grew tired of playing in the empty Opry House. They thought that since they were mice, no humans would want to hear them sing or see them play. They were very sad and did not want to have a band if they could not play to an audience.

Huxley's friends decided to move out of the Grand Ole Opry House and give up on their dream of being musicians. This saddened Huxley, who decided to stay at the Opry House and continue to play his banjo.

Huxley spent his days writing songs, learning how to play other instruments, playing his beloved banjo, and singing. Each night that there was a show, Huxley watched and sang along with the music, strumming his banjo.

When the show ended, Huxley climbed onto the stage and sang his own songs. He stared out into the empty seats and dreamed of them being filled!

Huxley knew that if he really wanted something, he could make it happen. He knew even though he was a mouse, that he would be a country music superstar one day, if he did not give up on his dream.

But as the days passed, Huxley became lonely in the big Opry House all by himself. He was sad that he did not have his friends there to keep him company or to play music with him.

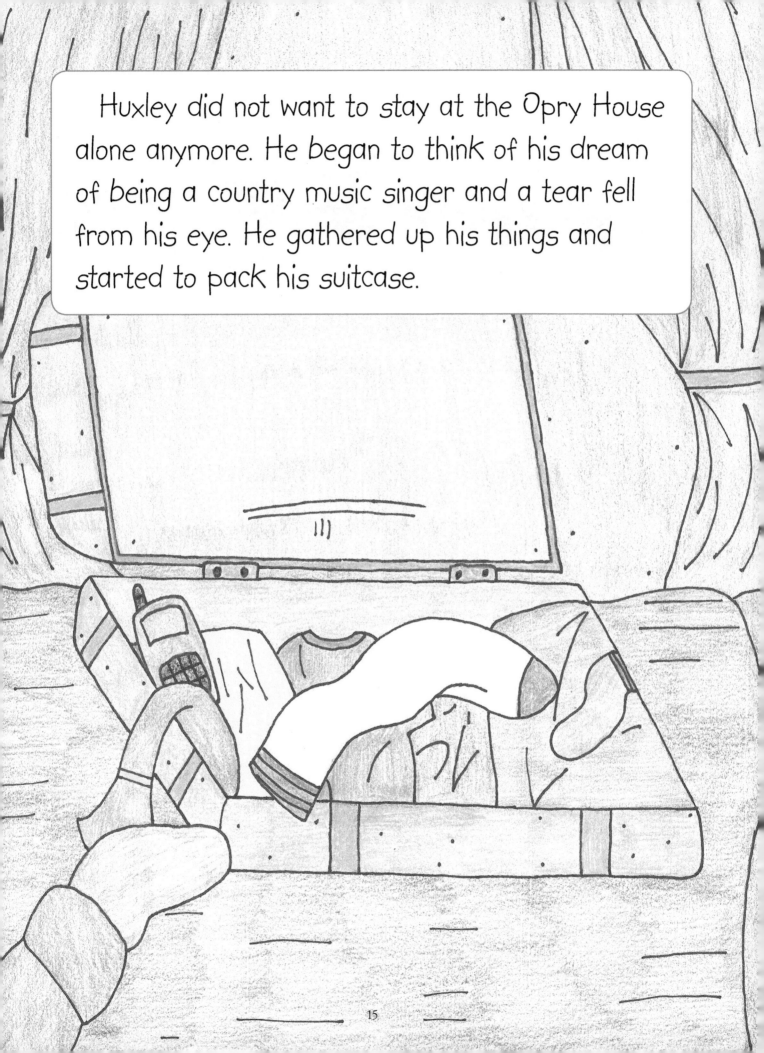

Huxley did not want to stay at the Opry House alone anymore. He began to think of his dream of being a country music singer and a tear fell from his eye. He gathered up his things and started to pack his suitcase.

Huxley shut his suitcase, threw his banjo over his shoulder, and began to walk away from the stage and into the hallway. As he walked, he hummed a sad little tune.

Huxley's humming was interrupted by the sound of a loud motor. He knew it was the sound of a tour bus and he became curious of who might be there. He climbed onto a shelf and peeked around the corner.

Huxley watched as a smiling blonde haired lady joyfully entered the Opry House. She looked very familiar to Huxley and he tried to recall where he had seen her before. However, he was distracted, when from the corner of his eye, he saw something move in her purse.

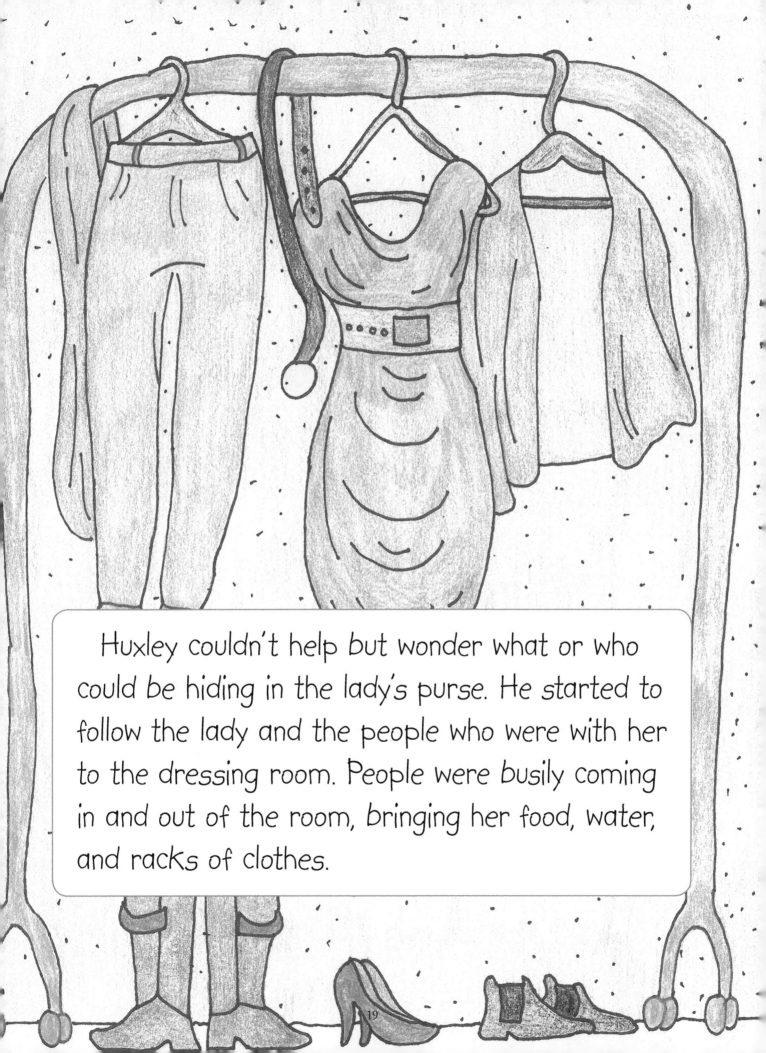

Huxley couldn't help but wonder what or who could be hiding in the lady's purse. He started to follow the lady and the people who were with her to the dressing room. People were busily coming in and out of the room, bringing her food, water, and racks of clothes.

Huxley knew the room was filled with too many people for him to investigate the purse. He decided to come back later that night when there were less people in the room who might see him. In the meantime, Huxley wandered off and started strumming his banjo.

Later that night, Huxley returned to the dressing room. The lady had changed into a blue sparkly outfit and was getting her hair and make-up done. The ladies in the room were talking and laughing and did not see Huxley enter the room and walk past them.

Huxley saw the silver purse that the lady had carried earlier that day. It was lying on the ground next to some high heeled shoes, scarves, and jewelry. Huxley walked over to it and looked inside. It was empty!

Huxley couldn't believe the purse was empty. He was sure that he saw something move in it earlier. Part of him was hoping it was another mouse who could keep him company. But now he thought that he was so lonely, he must have just imagined it moving.

Huxley sadly turned and started to walk away, tripping over the heel of a tall red high heel shoe.

All of a sudden he heard a voice cry, "Oh my goodness! Are you real or am I dreaming?" When he looked down he couldn't believe his little eyes. It was a mouse who had been asleep in the red high heel shoe.

The little mouse jumped up and introduced herself.

"Hi, I'm Hazel!" She exclaimed! I was just taking a nap before watching the show. Huxley finally found the words to say:

"Hello, I'm Huxley. It's nice to meet you."

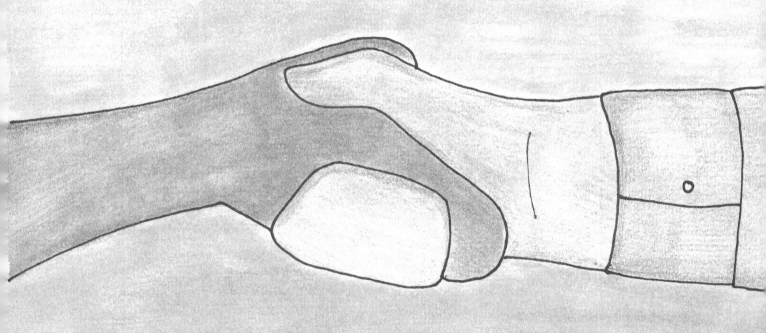

"How did you get here?" Huxley asked.

"Well I climbed into a shiny silver purse, which wound up on a tour bus and the bus came here." Hazel explained. "I am a singer and I'm going to be famous one day!" She added.

"I sing too!" Huxley said.

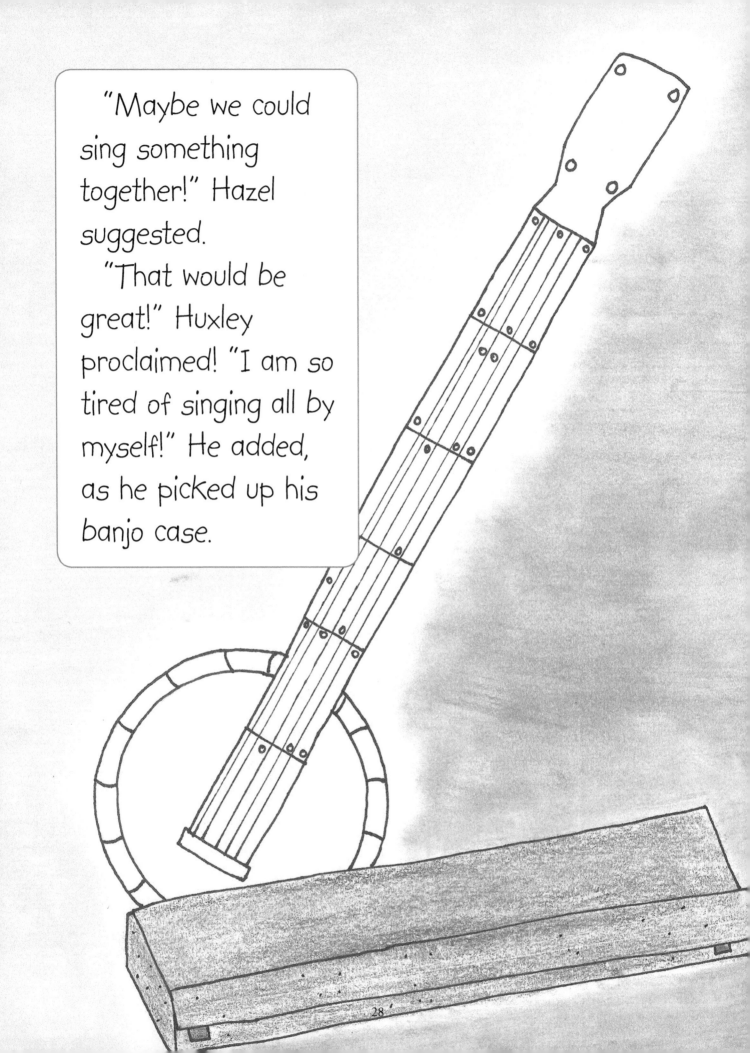

"Maybe we could sing something together!" Hazel suggested.

"That would be great!" Huxley proclaimed! "I am so tired of singing all by myself!" He added, as he picked up his banjo case.

Huxley and Hazel headed to the stage to see if anyone had arrived for the show yet.

The curtain was already up and the spotlights were on, but they were relieved to see that it was still early and there was no one there. So they climbed onto the stage.

Huxley began to strum the chords to his favorite country song on his banjo.

"I love that song!" Hazel squealed!

"Me too!" Huxley agreed.

30

Hazel began to sing along as Huxley played his banjo and tapped his boot along to the beat.

They sang the entire song and when they finished they took a bow. All of a sudden they heard someone clapping behind them. They turned around to see the lady in the sparkly blue outfit who would be performing on that same stage in just a few minutes!

"Wow!" The Lady exclaimed. "That was absolutely amazing!"

"Thank you so much!" Huxley and Hazel said excitedly.

The lady smiled and asked them, "How would y'all like to open up the show for me tonight?"

"Us?" Huxley asked.

"Wow!" He added.

"We'd love to!" Hazel squealed!

Soon the seats filled up with people and Huxley and Hazel got on stage. When the curtain rose, the people were a little shocked to see mice on the stage. Huxley and Hazel started the show with their favorite song.

The audience loved their performance! There was tons of singing along, clapping, and cheering which made Huxley and Hazel so happy!

Huxley and Hazel stepped to the side to watch their new friend's show. She was an amazing performer and Hazel sang along as she performed.

After the show, the lady invited Huxley and Hazel on to her tour bus. They followed her excitedly! The lady asked, "Would y'all like to come on tour with me and sing at all of my shows?"

"We'd love to!" Huxley shouted, knowing that his dreams were finally coming true! "I knew all my dreams would come true if I believed they would, worked hard, and followed my heart!" "Absolutely!" Hazel agreed as they smiled and hugged their new friend.

From that moment on, Huxley and Hazel were country music superstars, loving every minute of it! So set your sights high and never ever give up on your dreams!

CPSIA information can be obtained
at www.ICGtesting.com
Printed in the USA
LVHW07s1029221018
594371LV00010B/203/P

9 781546 250364